OF

CW00736269

Titles in Between The Lines:

HOPE AND TRUTH
DANIEL BLYTHE

KISS THE SKY
DANIEL BLYTHE

REFUGEE KID
CATHERINE BRUTON

ALONE
TIM COLLINS

COUNTY LINES
DONNA DAVID

ANNIE
TOMMY DONBAVAND

MESSAGE ALERT
ANN EVANS

PROMISE ME
ANN EVANS

OFFSIDE
IAIN McLAUGHLIN

SILENT VALLEY
CLIFF McNISH

SUCKER PUNCH
EMMA NORRY

MADE
KATE ORMAND

NOWHERE
KATE ORMAND

NO ESCAPE
JACQUELINE RAYNER

SIREN SONG
JACQUELINE RAYNER

THE CELL
JENNI SPANGLER

Badger Publishing Limited, Oldmedow Road, Hardwick Industrial Estate, King's Lynn PE30 4JJ

Telephone: 01438 791037

www.badgerlearning.co.uk

OFFSIDE

IAIN McLAUGHLIN

Offside ISBN 978-1-78837-445-3

Publisher / Senior Editor: Danny Pearson
Editor: Claire Wood
Copyeditor: Cheryl Lanyon
Designer: Bigtop Design Ltd
Cover: © Peter Muller / Getty Images

4 6 8 10 9 7 5

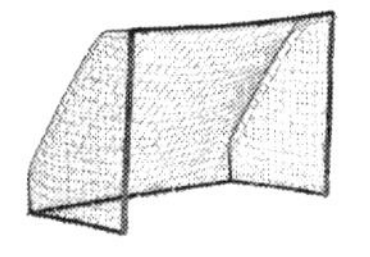

OFFSIDE

August 7

What do I need this journal for? They want me to write in it because Mum died? That's stupid, yeah? Writing stuff in a notebook won't bring Mum back. You've got to be an idiot to think it will.

August 8

Nadia thinks I'm an idiot. She reckons I should use this journal. She thinks it'll be good for me to write down how I feel. Why? I talk to her about it.

It's not that I don't like talking about Mum, it's that I don't like talking about her not being here. Every time I talk about her I have to remember she's gone. I just don't want to remember that. It's hard enough without being reminded constantly.

Nadia is usually right about stuff but I think she's wrong this time. I'll do it, but only because she wants me to.

August 10

Should I write this? Well, here goes. I feel guilty because I'm happy with Nadia. It feels wrong. I should be thinking about Mum but I'm thinking about Nadia instead. I feel guilty about that. I can't talk to nobody about it neither. Wait. That should be 'I can't talk to anybody about it either'. Mum hated it when I got grammar wrong.

I can't talk to Dad about me and Nadia. It wouldn't be fair to him, me getting with Nadia while he's getting over Mum dying. I can't talk to Naz either. He's my best mate but Nadia's his twin sister. She doesn't want him to know yet. He is either going to go totally cray-cray or think we're family already or something. Whatever he does, it'll be weird to begin with.

I'm not writing cray-cray again. It looks stupid written down.

August 12

Football training starts next week. I don't know if I want to do it. It's great that a Championship club thinks I'm worth developing at their academy, but I didn't enjoy last year so much. It wasn't just because Mum was ill, but that everybody was so serious about training. Naz would be gutted if I didn't play though. He's got this dream we're both going to get picked up by a Premier League team. A couple of scouts looked at us last year and said they would come back this season. I bet they say that to everybody.

August 13

I talked to Naz about football training today. Well, I asked what he thought about it and then I listened all afternoon. He can't wait for the season to start. I don't want to let him down.

August 15

Nadia thinks I should play this season. If I don't it will disappoint Naz, and Dad will feel really let down. He always wanted to make it in football but he didn't quite get there. He's desperate for me to get a career out of the game. Nadia thinks playing will be a good distraction for me. She might be right.

August 17

I think Nadia and I just had our first argument. I'm not happy keeping it secret that we're seeing each other. She doesn't want Naz to know as she thinks their parents will find out. I know he can keep a secret. I can't tell her about that, though. I shouldn't even write about it here.

August 20

I didn't enjoy lying to Naz about where I was yesterday. I told him I had some family stuff to do. I was with Nadia, just hanging out. Mum wouldn't like me hiding the truth from Naz. She wouldn't like that I haven't told Dad about Nadia either.

August 22

I had a long talk with Dad today. One of the men at work said something racist and his boss wouldn't do anything about it. I bet everybody who isn't white knows how it feels. We all get it. Naz and Nadia get it as well.

Dad cheered up when he started talking about football. He showed me old pictures of him when he was playing. Those shorts were ridiculous! My boxers are bigger than them. Dad was a good player and he really wanted to make it as a professional, but he says he wasn't good enough. He thinks I'm better than he was. I'm glad talking about football made him happy.

August 23

Nadia and I saw the new Marvel movie this afternoon. It was pretty good.

Naz has worked out that I've got a girlfriend so we're going to have to tell him soon. Nadia's going to study law when she finishes school. I always told Mum I wanted to be an architect. I still do. Although Dad would be heartbroken if I didn't have a career in football. I'm also not sure about leaving Dad on his own if I went to university.

It's not for a few years yet, but it's just him and me now. And university costs a lot of money, too. Do I want to start out with £50,000 in student debt?

I could just be making excuses so that I don't have to study for my exams. It's going to be really hard mixing football and studying this year.

August 24

We've got a new player in the squad. Todd Maldon. I don't like him. I don't know him, but I don't like him. There's something in the way he looks at people that's just nasty. I don't like it.

August 25

Naz doesn't like Todd either. Todd was talking to two other guys in the team and they were all talking about Naz and me. We could tell from how they looked at us and laughed in a sneaky way. I can guess whatever they said was stupid, and it certainly wasn't nice. I didn't hear what it was, but Naz did. He wouldn't tell me what they'd said as he knows I've got a short temper. He just changed the subject.

August 26

School started today.

I'd been looking forward to it. It was supposed to be me getting back to my normal life.

Nobody was horrible or anything. People either didn't know what to say about Mum or they were really kind. I don't know which was worse. The ones who avoided me made me feel like I had the plague. The ones who did talk and ask questions were just trying to be nice, but they all asked the same things. I had to talk about Mum dying and think about it again and again. All I really wanted was to get some normal back in my day.

The teachers were pretty good. Most of them caught me before class and asked if I was OK and if I needed anything. I won't get special treatment, but they did offer to arrange homework and stuff around anything I needed — counselling or anything like that. I said I just wanted to get back to ordinary life.

Truth is, I don't want to see a counsellor. Dad has offered a few times and he always asks why when I turn it down. I don't need some shrink in my head. That would mean there was something wrong with me, yeah? Well, there's nothing wrong with me. I know Dad's trying to help. It's like the people at school or in the community that want to help. I just want them to stop talking about it.

September 6

I haven't written in this for a bit.

I quit the team today. I really tried not to. I didn't want to let Dad down, but I just couldn't take any more of it. It hasn't been the same since Naz suddenly stopped playing a week or so ago. He won't tell me why he quit, but I reckon it must be something to do with Maldon and his bullying mates. I hate to think what they might have said or done to Naz. It must have been something really bad to cause him to give up what he loves.

Today was the last straw.

They put bananas in my locker. Bananas and monkey-nuts.

I went for them. I couldn't help myself. I just wanted to rip their heads off. Big Jordie caught me and it took him and Miggsy to stop me. I'd have hurt Maldon if I'd got hold of him. I just put my stuff in my bag and left. I'm not going back.

I'll tell Dad tomorrow, I can't tell him tonight. I can't look at him being disappointed. I told Naz. I talked to Nadia as well, on face time. That made me feel a bit better.

September 7

Dad knows I quit the team. They phoned him early this morning and now they want to see us both at 11am. Great. They're dragging me back in there just so they can kick me out. Too late,

I already quit. Dad was disappointed. I saw it in his eyes. He asked if I was sure, and I said I was. He didn't try to change my mind. He said we should blow off the meeting and just go for a burger or something.

Later

OK. So, I didn't expect this to happen!

Dad didn't exactly blow off the meeting. He cancelled by text then switched off our phones. We played a couple of frames of snooker and it turns out I'm the worst snooker player in the world. Dad's the second worst. They make it look really easy on TV. They get through a frame in ten minutes, yeah? We needed two hours to finish two frames. It didn't matter though, as it was just fun.

John Baxter, my team's coach, was waiting for us outside the flat when we got home. Mr Baxter asked why we had cancelled the meeting. I remember exactly what Dad said. "Cal already quit the team. You can't kick him out."

You know what I realised? Dad had my back. He wanted me to play but he still had my back. He wasn't going to let anybody have a go at me.

Baxter looked confused and explained that they weren't going to kick me out because I hadn't done anything wrong. He said they've suspended Todd Maldon and two other members of the team for racially unacceptable behaviour aimed at me, Naz and three other members of the team.

Well, that was a surprise.

Apparently, Miggsy and Big Jordie went to Baxter and made a complaint about what Todd and his friends had done in my locker. They took pictures and they left two of the bigger guys in the team to guard the locker while they went to him. Baxter found the bananas and the nuts and started an investigation straight away.

We'd thought that today's meeting was to kick me out. But it turns out it was a meeting to get our side of things.

Dad was a bit sheepish, but Baxter was nice about it. He explained that they haven't finished the investigation yet, but they think they'll be throwing Todd and his friends out. He said it's up to us whether we report it to the police.

I didn't expect the club to back us. I thought they'd be like other places and hide from it. Nobody ever wants to take racists head on.

Why am I so grateful that the club did the right thing, though? They just treated us like humans and I think I need to feel gratitude. That's what makes me angry. Racism happens so much, I just expect people to react in the worst way. I'm glad the club backed us. I shouldn't be surprised, I should expect it. We should all expect it.
But we don't.

Naz and I have to go in to the club tomorrow to make statements. I'm glad they supported us. But I still don't know how I feel about going back.

September 8

Todd Maldon and his mates got kicked out of the club this afternoon. None of them were there when we went in to give a statement. All three are gone now. Out.

The club apologised to Naz and me. They want us to go back and play. I'm still angry but I think I owe it to them to go back. Not to the club; they just did the right thing. It's Big Jordie and the rest of the team I owe really. They made the complaint and got Maldon and his mates hit with a misconduct hearing. Almost everybody in the team gave evidence about how Maldon acted. They called him out on what he did, and they all said he was racist. I also owe the team because they hung about to the end of the meeting to make sure Naz and I were OK.

Later

Baxter asked again if we want to make a complaint to the police about Maldon. I'm pretty sure I do. I don't know about Naz. Maldon shouldn't just be able to walk away after what he did.

September 9

Dad's glad I'm going back to the football team, but I haven't heard from Naz since yesterday. I texted him a few times. He must be busy.

Later

Naz is coming back to the club, but he doesn't want to involve the police. That sounds like his dad. Mr Afzal is old-school and he doesn't like dragging the authorities into things. He thinks it's better to just get on with life. Naz was a bit off when I spoke to him. Maybe Nadia knows why.

September 10

Naz knows about me and Nadia. She told him. That's why he doesn't want to report Maldon to the police. The papers would be interested in the story because we're in football. Naz is worried the papers would also find out and write about me and Nadia, and that would cause trouble at home.

I don't know if it's me personally, or if her family just aren't ready for her to have a boyfriend. Her mum will be cool with it but Mr Afzal won't be.

And I don't think he's ever going to be ready for Naz to take home a boyfriend. Luckily Naz is very good at keeping secrets.

I think Naz's mum might have an idea he's gay. She's asked me a few times if he has a 'girlfriend or anyone special' at school. She wasn't being nosy and I don't think she cares which sex Naz fancies. She just wants him to be happy. She's pretty cool.

I hope she's still cool if she catches her daughter snogging my face off.

September 12

We got stopped by the police today. Me, Nadia and Naz. We were just walking along and they stopped us. All we were doing was walking home. Mum always told me to stay calm if I got stopped by the police. Don't show them any signs of aggression. Don't give them a reason to cause you trouble. My skin's the only reason they needed.

They looked in our bags and asked questions about where we were going and what we were doing. When they were finished they just sent us on our way. They didn't explain why we'd been stopped, and they didn't apologise or say thanks. They just moved us on.

You know what it reminded me of? The way they shift cattle on those stupid Sunday TV shows about farming. It was like we weren't human. We weren't the same as the white kids who were wandering past in hoodies, shouting insults at them. They made me feel like we weren't as good as other people. Or, rather, they made me feel like **they** didn't think I was as good as other people.

I totally get why Mum always said to cooperate. It might have been much worse if I'd gone off on one. Understanding it doesn't make me feel any better. It makes me angry that Mum told me to accept it; and angry that she's not here so I can tell her I'm angry with her. I'm angry with her for getting sick, and I'm angry with her for dying and leaving us.

I hate this journal.

September 17

I told myself that I wasn't going to write in this thing again.

I try not to think about Mum. I mean, I try not to think about her dying. I try to just remember the good things and the happy times. I really try, but it's hard not to miss her. It's just that the thoughts come out of nowhere. I can be OK, listening to music, watching a vlog or something. My head is totally in what I'm doing and then it just hits me again that Mum's dead. For the first few weeks that was all I thought about. Now I'm getting on with things, but I suddenly remember it all over again and it hurts every time. I know it's affecting how I think about other things. I just can't help it.

September 20

The West Area Cup starts this week. It's got eight teams, so that means quarter-finals, semi-finals and then a final. The winners go into the national play-offs later in the season.

The Cup is kind of a big deal. Most of us are from Championship clubs but there are a couple of Premier League teams involved. Scouts from all over watch these games. They're the kind of matches that make the scouts and managers decide if players are worth spending time on. It's not just about skill, it's temperament too. If you can handle the pressure, they'll be interested. If you fall apart, you'll be out the door. There's a lot of stress and pressure in football. A lot of money, too. The clubs always remind us how much they have spent on us.

One of the coaches caught Kevin Hackett skipping training last season. They were brutal with him and reminded him how much they'd invested in him.

He quit at the end of last season, saying he couldn't study and do football as well. I honestly don't know if I can, either.

September 21

Training is hard. They are really pushing us. I'm going to sleep for a week.

September 23

Scored the best goal of my life today! Pity it was only in training, but it was beautiful. We played a one-two to get to the last defender, then I passed it on to Naz. He had his back to the goal. He rolled his shoulder and body to go right but he flicked the ball to the left. That put it in my path. One touch and I buried it in the bottom corner.

That wasn't just a goal. That was art. I'm like Banksy in football boots!

September 26

First game is tomorrow so I'm keeping this short. I need some sleep. I'm going to tell Dad about me and Nadia in the morning.

September 27

Dad knew about me and Nadia. Seriously, man, does anybody not know?

Later

Easy 6-2 win for us. Three goals for me, two for Naz. Big Jordie got the other goal. He's a central defender but he scored with a great back heel after a corner. Big Jordie's Scottish. From Glasgow, I think, and his accent gets hard to understand when he's excited. To be fair, I sometime think EastEnders should have subtitles.

I'm putting off writing what's bothering me…

We got monkey chants at the game. The crowd was about five or six hundred. For us, that's great. There was no segregation keeping the fans apart, so I don't know who made the noise, but they were with the opposition team. Every time Naz, or me, or anybody who isn't white got the ball, the monkey noises started.

I told the referee about it before half time. I expected him to do something, but he didn't. He did nothing. All he said was that we should ignore it and play on. The rest of the team were great; they kept coming to us to make sure we were OK.

Scoring the goals was the best way I could hit back at them. Although those chants stopped me enjoying today like I should have.

September 29

Today was good. No football training or anything. I just really enjoyed school. We got a new project to design a building. Any kind of building is OK. Miss Letts thinks I'll design a sports stadium. Yeah, right.

We need to build tens of thousands of houses every year. Somebody has to design and build them. That's what I want to do. Mum worked in the housing department for the Council. She helped find houses for people so that they didn't have to live in B&Bs or temporary housing. If I can design houses to help people it would be like I was helping Mum. It would be like I could do something for her and that would sort of keep her near me. Yeah, I'm going to design houses for this project. Good houses that people could be proud to live in. I'm going to enjoy this.

Nadia gets why it matters to me. She's always known that she wants to be a lawyer. Since Mum died, I've been thinking more about becoming an architect, although I know Dad would rather I become a professional footballer.

October 1

Training today was OK. I kind of didn't want to go. The last few sessions have been a bit boring. There has always been a lot of repetition in football training. You do the same things over and over until they are 100 per cent right. Sometimes it's fun; sometimes it's not. My mind has been on my project, and on Nadia, recently.

We have a game on Saturday and we're away overnight. It's a friendly, but we have to treat it like it's a Cup game. It kind of feels like being a real footballer.

October 2

Another good day. School was boring but training was fun, then Dad took me, Naz and Nadia for a burger. Do serious athletes eat burger and chips?

October 3

I'm not taking this journal away with me to the match. I'll fill it in when I get back tomorrow.

October 4

We won 4-1! Two goals for me, plus an assist with a cross onto Naz's head. I owed him that. He gave me my second on a plate.

I learned a bad thing yesterday — Naz snores. Seriously, man. I had to plug my buds in to play music so I didn't hear him. It was brutal. How can anybody sleep in a house with him?

October 6

I picked up a dead leg in training today. It's fine but it's got me a day off tomorrow — bonus! I'm going to see a film with Nadia.

October 7

Going to a film with Nadia turned into seeing a film with Nadia and her mum. What's that about? We didn't invite her. She just invited herself to join us. I'm not sure when her mum found out about us, but I spent most of the film worrying about whether she'll tell Nadia's dad. Plus, there was zero per cent chance of any misbehaving with her mum there. She insisted on paying for everything, so that was something, I suppose.

Does that mean she likes me, or not?

October 8

The semi is on Saturday. Mr Baxter is putting us through our drills for that game. He's been watching the other team. Their defenders are big but they're slow. He wants us to drop deep and make them follow us so we can then spin and run behind them, while our midfield play the ball over the top of them to us. We spent an hour on that today. I'm dizzy after all that spinning.

October 9

Same drill at training as last time. The defenders were away doing their own practice. They'll be up against a big striker. It's more physical than skill with him, so they're working on coping with him.

The last hour was different. Mr Baxter sat the squad down and we thought he was going to talk tactics. Wrong.

The team we're playing at the weekend has a really bad reputation. Their supporters are known for being awful to opposition players of colour. All the usual racist garbage these morons always use. I've been called everything, ever since I can remember. Black this, black that. The really bad stuff as well. I won't write it down. They don't get to make me write that filth down in my own journal. Baxter wanted us to know that we could sit the game out if we wanted. There are five of us of colour in the team. Baxter said he had asked for the game to be moved but the other team objected. He said it was up to us if we play or not.

It's a semi and a lot of big teams will be watching. We're all signed to our team but not everybody is going to make it here. We need to be seen by other teams as well.

I don't want to play but I have to. We all feel the same way.

October 10

The game is tomorrow. I'm glad we're not staying away overnight this time. I think coming home will be the most fun part of the day.

Dad's coming and so are Nadia and her family and a lot of the other parents. Nadia's mum offered Dad a lift. With all three parents together, I'm sure Mr Afzal will know about Nadia and me by kick-off. Maybe I'll get lucky and he'll get me with a sliding tackle and take me out before we start.

October 11

Good news first. We won 3-1. One by me, one by Naz and a header by Big Jordie from a corner. We're in the final!

Nadia's dad didn't kill me. He scowled at me a bit before kick-off but that was it. He gets on with Dad, which helps.

The bad news — the abuse was shocking. We've all faced it before. We don't accept it, but we learn to get through it. We don't ignore it; we just deal with it. But I really struggled to deal with it today. I got the usual — the monkey chants and all that rubbish. Naz got it worse. He was the only Asian guy on the pitch and they really went for him. Terrorist stuff, shouting about burkas and bombs.

It's hard to focus on a game with that going on. I knew where Dad was, with the Afzals. I found out after the game that Nadia and her mum had stopped Mr Afzal from confronting the scumbags. Dad was ready to back Mr Afzal up.

I'm glad nothing happened. I also kind of wish they had kicked off. I'm just happy we beat that team and don't have to go back there. We're going to the final. They're not.

October 12

Normally we don't have training the day after a game but we did today. The big names upstairs wanted to congratulate us on making the final. That was the Chairperson, the first-team manager, the captain and some of the first-team players as well. It was really weird having them ask us how we felt and how we enjoyed the game. It's strange talking to them like we're real players too.

That took the edge off how angry we were about the game. The Chairperson told us who we'll be playing in the final. She's so chuffed we'll be playing against a really big Premier League team, and said she wants us to be an example to the rest of the club. We felt three metres high.

That lasted until we found out that Todd Maldon and the other two scumbags our team had let go for racism are now playing for the team we'll be playing in the final. I hadn't heard they'd been picked up by another club. I couldn't believe a team that big had signed them.

October 14

Naz was off school today. He didn't answer my messages. Nadia says he's just not feeling great.

Training was fitness today, nothing skill-related. We move on to plans for the final later in the week.

October 15

My school project is nearly done and the houses look great. I should be pleased with it. I am, I suppose. I did an OK job.

It's stupid but playing against those three racists is bothering me. They keep creeping into my head and spoiling everything. They should be gone from the game; they shouldn't be in a final.

October 16

I met Naz at lunchtime. He says he's dropping out of football for good this time because he's been getting more hassle. Not from his dad or anything. Somebody spray-painted TERRORIST on his dad's car last night. Naz has lived here all his life, but now he says he feels like he doesn't belong in his own country. He also said he might feel different tomorrow, but he's just sick today.
I don't blame him.

Later

Nadia's upset by that paint on her dad's car as well. She hides it better than Naz, but it hurts her. She held my hand a lot tighter when we went past a loud group of lads. They weren't doing anything except joking, but she's nervous. She's usually completely together but this has got to her.

October 17

I got a banana through the post at the club today.

A banana.

I can't write about that. I just can't.

October 18

The club passed the banana to the police yesterday and I had to answer a load of questions. It's obvious who did this. The minute Todd Maldon is anywhere near us again, we get this garbage. Naz's dad got it, and now me.

October 20

The police said that Maldon and his mates deny everything.

Big surprise.

The police can't prove anything.

Brilliant.

October 22

Franklyn, one of my other teammates, got a bunch of racial stuff sent to his phone. Pictures of gorillas, saying they're his family. That was the mild end of what he got. The club contacted the police again.

October 24

No word from the police about Franklyn's messages. If the bullies used a VPN to hide where they were, then there's a good chance the police won't find them at all.

October 25

It was the training ground's turn today. D****** GO HOME was sprayed on the wall. I'm not writing the full word. Whoever did it knew the club buildings and they knew where they wouldn't be caught by cameras.

Naz asked what it would be like if either of us actually made it in football. We'd have to deal with this EVERY DAY. He talked about the stuff

Danny Rose and Raheem Sterling have been through. Do I want to deal with that every single day?

I don't. I enjoy football but it should be fun. Maybe I should just focus on a good job and forget football.

October 26

I'm really thinking about quitting the team. There's the final though — but what's the point if I'm just going to be miserable? Why should I let people abuse me? Football's not worth that.

I'm done with it.

I quit.

Later

Dad's disappointed but he's trying not to show it. He said, "It's your choice. I'll back you, whatever."

He's supporting me but he wishes I wasn't quitting. I feel like I'm letting him down.

October 27

I told Mr Baxter today. He asked me to think about it. He said people would give anything for the opportunity and talent I have. Would they give anything for the abuse that goes with it though?

I told Naz and Nadia as well. She was worried I'd regret it. Well, it's done anyway.

Franklyn texted me — he's quit as well. He's pretty down and he isn't sure he made the right decision. We're meeting after school tomorrow.

October 28

Something weird happened today. Nadia, Naz and I met Franklyn in the park after school. A bunch of kids were there with a ball and we just sort of joined in. We really enjoyed it. No hassle or abuse, only fun. We all just played because we felt like it. Nadia played as well.

She's a poacher and she scored a load of goals, half of them nicked from me.

It was really good fun.

October 29

Playing in the park yesterday has got to me. I enjoyed it. I wanted to play. I still want to play.

Naz wants to play as well because he enjoyed it. So did Franklyn.

We were all angry that we'd had our love of the game stolen from us. It's not about football. It's about them being scum and using football as a way to be scum. We're not going to let them take our game away from us.

We're going to ask Baxter if we can play.

October 30

We're back in the squad. Maybe not in the team, but in the squad. I'm having second thoughts already. This could be really stupid but I'm going to do it.

November 1

My messages here are getting shorter. It's nerves.

I'm not sure if I'm most nervous about the match or the stuff around it.

November 2

Part of me wants to put Todd Maldon into the crowd on my first tackle. I can do it too. I'm bigger than him and I'm stronger than him. It's horrible that I want to hurt him.

Later

Baxter started me, Naz and Franklyn in the game. I didn't expect that, but it felt good. None of the team shook hands with Maldon at the start. Big Jordie left Maldon hanging with his hand out and we all just blanked him.

It wasn't a great game but we were the better team. They were nasty and deliberately stood on feet and ankles to try to hurt us. They dived, too.

We were 1-0 at half time. Naz put me through and I slid it under their keeper. We should have had more, but their goalie had an amazing game. Maldon kept clear of Naz and me. He dived a few times and picked up fouls for his team, but that was all he did in the first half.

About ten minutes into the second half, one of their lot kicked the ball to Maldon in our penalty box, before backing into Big Jordie and throwing himself flat. The ref gave the other team a penalty. It was a joke! Big Jordie didn't touch him. The other guy cheated for the penalty and they ended up scoring because of it.

There had been noises from the crowd from the start — all from their end. I don't get it. They have black players in their team, but they still made monkey noises when we got the ball, or shouted "Bomb!" when it went to Naz.

I had to take a throw at their end. One of them threw a banana and it hit me on the head. The ref saw it and stopped the match. He showed it to the police — they've got cameras on the crowd here. A couple of the other team's supporters got dragged out a few minutes later. Big Jordie said he'd lead the team off if we wanted it. This is our game though: we play it because we love it. Walking off would be a statement, but winning would be a bigger statement. I don't know if it was the right thing to do but it felt right at the time. We played on.

With ten minutes left, Naz slid me through on the right. I dinked it to the back post. Franklyn arrived like a train and his header almost took the net away.

We won, 2-1. We beat Maldon and we played fair to do it.

We blanked them totally after the game and even Baxter didn't shake their manager's hand.

We won!

November 3

We're in the paper, on the back page with a huge picture. Nobody has ever smiled as big as Franklyn in that picture. Everybody cheered us when we got back to the training ground with the trophy. The kids in the younger teams looked at us the same way we look at the first team.

A few of the first team were at the game and so was the manager. A couple of us have been called up to train with them for a few weeks. I don't think Franklyn will be coming with us because one of the big London teams wants to talk to him. I'm so pleased for him.

Later

I'm in a good place at the moment. I've got my first medal. I know it's not the World Cup but it's mine. We won and we won the right way. I don't know if I'm going to make it in football and I don't know if I really want this as my life.

I'll play as long as I enjoy it and, if I need to choose between football and studying, I'll decide when I have to.

For now, I'm just going to enjoy being happy.
I know that's what Mum would want.

THE END

ABOUT THE AUTHOR

Iain McLaughlin lives in his hometown of Dundee in Scotland, in a house filled with books. He has written more than a dozen novels and around 50 plays for radio or audio, many about popular characters and series, including James Bond, Doctor Who and Sherlock Holmes. For a time, he was the editor of the *Beano* comic.

Helplines and online support

Here are some excellent resources which can explain any difficult questions you might have:

www.kickitout.org

www.stonewall.org.uk

www.childline.org.uk

www.anti-bullyingalliance.org.uk

www.nspcc.org.uk

www.youngminds.org.uk